Farmer
Boy Days

THE LITTLE HOUSE
CHAPTER BOOKS

Adapted from the Little House books
by Laura Ingalls Wilder
Illustrated by Renée Graef

THE ADVENTURES OF LAURA & JACK
PIONEER SISTERS
ANIMAL ADVENTURES
SCHOOL DAYS
LAURA & NELLIE
FARMER BOY DAYS

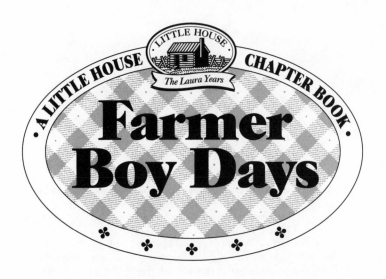

A LITTLE HOUSE CHAPTER BOOK ·
LITTLE HOUSE
The Laura Years

Farmer Boy Days

LAURA INGALLS WILDER

illustrated by
RENÉE GRAEF

HarperCollins*Publishers*

Adaptation by Melissa Peterson.

HarperCollins®, ✎®, and Little House®
are trademarks of HarperCollins Publishers Inc.

Farmer Boy Days
Text adapted from *Farmer Boy*, text copyright 1933, copyright renewed 1961,
Roger Lea MacBride.
Illustrations copyright © 1998 by Renée Graef.
Copyright © 1998 by HarperCollins Publishers.
Library of Congress Cataloging-in-Publication Data
Farmer boy days [adapted from the Little house books] by Laura Ingalls
Wilder / illustrated by Renée Graef.
p.   cm. — (A Little house chapter book)
Text adapted from Farmer boy.
Summary: As he grows up on his family's farm in New York, Almanzo
Wilder dreams of having a colt of his own.
ISBN 0-06-027497-2 (lib. bdg.) — ISBN 0-06-442061-2 (pbk.)
1. Wilder, Almanzo—Juvenile fiction.   [1. Wilder, Almanzo—Fiction.
2. Farm life—New York (State)—Fiction.   3. Family life—New York
(State)—Fiction.   4. Horses—Fiction.   5. New York (State)—Fiction.]
I. Wilder, Laura Ingalls, 1867–1957. Farmer boy.   II. Graef, Renée, ill.
III. Series.
PZ7.F838235   1998   96-11649
[Fic]—DC21   CIP
                                                                    AC
2   3   4   5   6   7   8   9   10
❖

Contents

CHAPTER 1

The Horse-Barn

It was chore time at the Wilder farm in northern New York State. The winter air was still as ice. Almanzo's nose tingled in the cold as he trudged toward the Horse-Barn.

Almanzo was not quite nine years old. His sister Alice was ten, his other sister Eliza Jane was twelve, and his brother Royal was thirteen years old. They all lived on a farm with their mother and father.

Every day after school Eliza Jane and Alice helped Mother in the house. Royal

1

and Almanzo worked with Father in the barns.

The Horse-Barn was Almanzo's favorite place. He loved horses. He loved to watch them standing in their stalls, clean and sleek and gleaming brown. Their manes and tails were black. Almanzo's father had some of the best horses in New York.

The horses all knew Almanzo. Their ears pricked up and their eyes shone when they saw him. The sedate workhorses looked up from the hay they were munching. The three-year-olds came eagerly and thrust their heads out to nuzzle at him.

Their noses were soft as velvet. Their necks arched proudly and the black manes fell over them like a fringe. You could run your hand along those firm, curved necks, in the warmth under the mane.

 2

But Almanzo hardly dared to do it. He was not allowed to touch the beautiful three-year-olds. He could not go into their stalls, not even to clean them. Father would not let him handle the young horses or the frisky colts. Colts and young, un-broken horses, Father said, were very easy to spoil.

A boy who didn't know any better might scare a young horse. He might tease it or even hit it. That would ruin the horse. It would learn to bite and kick and hate people.

Almanzo did know better. He would never scare or hurt one of those beautiful colts. He would always be quiet and gentle. He would never startle a colt. He wouldn't ever shout at it, not even if it stepped on his foot.

But Father wouldn't believe this.

3

So Almanzo could only look longingly at the eager three-year-olds. He looked as long as he could, and then he hurried to do his chores.

He put work clothes on over his good school clothes. Father had already watered all the animals in the three barns. Now he was giving them their grain.

Royal and Almanzo grabbed pitchforks. They moved from stall to stall, cleaning out the dirty hay. They spread fresh hay to make clean beds for the animals. There were the cows and oxen in the Big Barn, and the hogs, sheep, and calves in the South Barn.

Two of the calves in the South Barn belonged to Almanzo. Their names were Star and Bright. Star had a white spot on his forehead, and Bright was a bright red all over.

 4

They came crowding to the bars when they saw Almanzo. They were young calves, not yet a year old. Their little horns were just beginning to grow hard in the soft hair by their ears. Almanzo gave them each a good scratching around the horns. The calves loved it, and they pushed their noses between the bars to lick Almanzo's hands.

Almanzo took a carrot from the cows' feed-box. He snapped little pieces off for Star and Bright. The calves tickled his hand with their rough tongues.

Then it was time to climb up to the haymows high in the barn. Royal and Almanzo scooped up hay with their pitch-forks and threw it into the mangers below. Almanzo could hear the crunch of all the animals eating. The hay smelled dusty-sweet. He could smell horses and cows

5

and the woolly smell of sheep.

And before the boys were finished, there was the good smell of warm milk foaming into Father's pail.

Almanzo climbed out of the haymow and put away his pitchfork. He took his own little milking stool to Blossom's stall. His hands were not yet strong enough to milk most of the cows, but he could milk Blossom and Bossy. They were good old cows who gave their milk easily. They hardly ever flicked him in the face with their swishing tails, or knocked over the pail with a hind foot.

He sat with the pail between his feet, and milked steadily. Left, right! Swish, swish! Milk streamed into the pail.

The barn cats came to sit purring at his feet. They were sleek and fat from eating mice. Every barn cat had large ears and a

long tail—sure signs of a good mouser. Day and night they patrolled the barns, keeping the rats and mice out of the grain.

Swish, swish! Almanzo finished milking Blossom and started on Bossy. Left, right, swish, swish! Before long the milkpail was full. Almanzo poured some of the

7

warm, fresh milk into pans for the cats. The cats purred as they lapped it up.

Father finished milking the rest of the cows. He went into Blossom's stall and sat down to strip the last drops of milk from her udder. Those last drops were the richest, creamiest parts of the milk. Not a drop must be missed.

But Father stood up again almost at once. Almanzo had got all the milk. Father checked Bossy, and again he stood up right away.

"You're a good milker, son," he told Almanzo.

Almanzo was too pleased to say a word. Now he could milk cows by himself. Father needn't strip them after him. Pretty soon, Almanzo knew, he would be milking the hardest milkers.

He couldn't wait.

 8

CHAPTER 2

Birthday Surprise

O ne cold morning, while Almanzo was eating his oatmeal, Father said something that made Almanzo look up in surprise. Today was his birthday! Almanzo had forgotten it. He was nine years old today.

"There's something for you in the woodshed," Father said.

Almanzo wanted to see it right away. But Mother said if he did not eat his breakfast he must be sick, and would have to take medicine.

Then he ate as fast as he could.

9

"Don't take such big mouthfuls," Mother scolded.

At last breakfast was over. Almanzo raced to the woodshed. There he found a little red calf-yoke! Father had made it of red cedar. It was strong and light.

"Yes, son," Father said, "you are old enough now to break the calves."

Almanzo did not have to go to school that day. He ran out to the barn, carrying the yoke. Father came behind him. Maybe, Almanzo thought, maybe if he did a good job breaking the calves, Father might let him help with the colts next year.

Star and Bright were in their warm stall in the South Barn. Their little red sides were sleek and silky. Almanzo always made sure they were properly brushed.

He went into the stall. The calves

 10

crowded against him, licking him with their rough tongues. They thought he had brought them carrots. They did not know he was going to teach them how to behave like big oxen.

Almanzo let down the bars of the stall. The calves followed him into the cold, snowy barnyard. Father showed him how to fit the yoke carefully onto their necks. The yoke would keep the calves lined up next to each other, side by side.

First they put one side of the yoke on Bright's neck. They fastened it in place with a wooden bow that fit under his head. Bright twisted his head a little to see what this strange thing was on his neck. But he trusted Almanzo and stood quietly.

Almanzo gave him a piece of carrot. Star heard him crunching it and came to get his share. Then Almanzo fastened the other end of the yoke around Star's neck, nudging him into place beside Bright.

Now Almanzo had a yoke of oxen! They stood side by side, ready to pull anything Almanzo fastened to the yoke, like a plow or a wagon. At least, they would be ready as soon as Almanzo broke them.

Breaking the calves meant he would teach them how to pull as a team, and how to follow his instructions. They must learn to start and stop and turn left or right when Almanzo said so.

Father tied a rope around Star's little nubs of horns. Almanzo took the rope and stood in front of the calves.

"Giddap!" he shouted.

Star's neck stretched out longer and longer. Almanzo pulled. Finally Star stepped forward. Bright snorted and pulled back. The yoke twisted Star's head

 12

around and stopped him. The two calves stood wondering what it was all about.

Father helped Almanzo push them till they stood side by side again.

"Well, son," Father said, "I'll leave you to figure it out." He went back to the barn.

It was then that Almanzo knew he really was old enough to do important things all by himself.

He stood in the snow and looked at the calves. They stared back at him with their wide, trusting eyes. How could he teach them what "Giddap!" meant? There wasn't any way to tell them. But he must find some way to make them understand that when he said, "Giddap!" they must walk straight ahead.

He had an idea. He went to the cows' feed-box and filled his pockets with carrots. When he came back, he stood as far in front of the calves as the rope around Star's horns would reach. He put his free hand into his pocket and shouted, "Giddap!"

Then he took a carrot out of his pocket.

Star and Bright came eagerly. They wanted that carrot. When they reached him, Almanzo shouted, "Whoa!" and they stopped for the carrot. He gave each of them a piece.

When they had eaten it, he backed away again and put his hand in his pocket.

"Giddap!"

In no time at all the calves had figured it out. They learned to start forward on "Giddap!" and stop on "Whoa!" They were behaving as well as grown-up oxen!

Then Father came to the door and said, "That's enough, son. Calves will stop minding you if you work them too hard at first. Besides, it's dinner-time."

Almanzo could hardly believe it. The whole morning had gone in a minute.

He lifted the yoke off the calves' necks and led them back to their warm stall. Father showed him how to wipe the yoke with wisps of clean hay. He must always keep it clean and dry, or the calves would

15

have sore necks.

In the Horse-Barn Almanzo stopped just a minute to look at the colts. He liked Star and Bright, but calves were clumsy compared with the slender, quick colts. Their ears moved swiftly as birds. They tossed their heads with a flutter of manes. Their eyes were full of spirit.

"I'd like to help break a colt," Almanzo said quietly.

"It's a man's job, son," Father said. "One little mistake will ruin a fine colt."

Almanzo knew Father was right, but still, he longed to work with the beautiful horses.

But it was exciting to be breaking his very own calves. He had worked hard that morning, and now he was very hungry. He followed Father back to the house, where Mother had dinner waiting.

After he had eaten, Mother asked him to fill the wood-box. Almanzo opened the woodshed door. He stood staring in surprise.

There, right before him, was a brand-new sled!

He could hardly believe it was for him. The calf-yoke was his birthday present. He asked, "Whose sled is that, Father? Is it—it isn't for me?"

Mother laughed. Father's eyes twinkled and he said, "Do you know any other nine-year-old that wants it?"

Almanzo's heart was soaring. A calf-yoke, and a new sled! It was the best birthday ever.

CHAPTER 3

Breaking the Calves

Every chance Almanzo got, he worked with the calves. He must keep training them, or they would forget all they had learned. On Saturday mornings he went eagerly to the barn and called them out into the frosty air.

He fitted the little yoke over their heads and fastened the bows around their necks. He tied the rope around Star's nubs of horns. He could do it by himself now. Father had only helped him that first time.

All morning he would lead the calves

around the barnyard. Star and Bright came eagerly when he yelled "Giddap!" They stopped when he said "Whoa!" and gobbled up the pieces of carrot from his woolly mittens.

Then, before he knew it, it would be noon, and time to stop. One afternoon Father helped him make a whip out of a supple tree branch. Almanzo could crack that whip as loudly as Father cracked his big blacksnake whip that was made of leather.

The whip was to help him teach Star and Bright to turn left and right. He never whipped them; he only waved the whip in the air in just the right way to make a sharp cracking sound. Almanzo knew you could never teach an animal anything if you struck it, or even if you shouted at it. He must always be gentle and patient

19

with the calves. Star and Bright must like him and trust him.

Soon he didn't even have to stand in front of them with the carrot anymore to get them to "Giddap!" and "Whoa!" Then he began working on left and right.

He taught them to go right when he said, "Gee!" And when he said, "Haw!" the calves must go left. Slowly they began to get the hang of it.

After a few Saturdays Star and Bright obeyed him perfectly. He did not need to crack the whip, because they obeyed his shout. But he cracked it anyway. It made such a fine, crisp sound in the frosty air.

One Saturday the French boys, Pierre and Louis, came to see Almanzo. They lived in little houses in the woods with their many brothers and sisters. Sometimes their fathers worked for Almanzo's father.

 20

Pierre and Louis watched while Almanzo showed off his calves in the barnyard. Star and Bright were behaving so well that Almanzo had a splendid idea.

He brought out his birthday sled and hitched it to the calf-yoke.

"Now, Louis, you get on the sled," he said excitedly.

"No, I'm biggest!" Pierre said. He pushed Louis back. "I get the first ride."

Almanzo shook his head. He was afraid the calves would try to run away when they felt the unfamiliar weight of the sled and rider behind them.

"Let Louis go first because he's lighter," Almanzo said.

"No," Louis mumbled. "I don't want to."

"Are you scared?" Almanzo asked.

"Yes, he's scared!" Pierre said.

21

"I am not," Louis said. "I just don't want to."

"He's scared," Pierre sneered.

"I am not, either!"

"You are!" Almanzo and Pierre said. They said Louis was a fraidy-cat. They said he was a baby. Pierre told him to go back to his mamma. So finally Louis sat down on the sled.

Almanzo cracked his whip and shouted, "Giddap!"

Star and Bright started—and stopped. They tried to turn around to see what was behind them.

But Almanzo said sternly, "Giddap!" again. This time the calves started and kept on going.

Almanzo walked beside them, cracking his whip and shouting "Gee!" He drove them clear around the barnyard.

 22

Pierre ran after the sled and got on, too. The calves behaved perfectly.

So Almanzo opened the barnyard gate.

Pierre and Louis quickly jumped off the sled.

"They'll run away!" Pierre said.

"I guess I know my own calves," Almanzo said. He cracked the whip. "Giddap!"

Almanzo drove the calves right out of the safe barnyard into the big, wide, glittering world beyond.

He shouted, "Haw!" and he shouted, "Gee!" He drove them past the house. He drove them out to the road. When he shouted, "Whoa!" they stopped.

Pierre and Louis were excited now. They piled onto the sled. Almanzo made them slide back so he could ride, too. He sat in front, with Pierre behind him and

23

Louis in back. Their legs stuck out stiffly at the sides.

Once more Almanzo proudly cracked his whip.

"Giddap!"

Up went Star's tail. Up when Bright's tail. Up went their heels. The sled bounced into the air.

And then everything happened all at once.

"Baw-aw-aw!" said Star.

"Baw-aw-aw-aw!" said Bright. Right in Almanzo's face were flying hoofs and swishing tails.

"Whoa!" yelled Almanzo. "Whoa!"

The calves kept baw-aw-awing. They ran down the snowy road, dragging the sled behind them. It was far swifter than sliding downhill. Trees and snow and calves' legs were all mixed up. Every time

 24

the sled came down Almanzo's teeth crashed together.

Bright was running faster than Star. They were going off the road. The sled was turning over!

"Haw! Haw!" Almanzo yelled. He wanted the calves to pull back toward the left, so the sled would stay on the road. "Haw!" He kept on yelling "Haw!" as he sailed headfirst into a snowbank.

His open mouth was full of snow. He spit it out and scrambled up.

Everything was still. The road was empty. The calves were gone. The sled was gone.

Pierre and Louis sat up in the snow. Louis was swearing in French. Pierre sputtered and wiped the snow from his face.

"*Sacre bleu!*" Pierre said. "I think you

say you drive your calves. They not run away, eh?"

Almanzo spotted something far down the road—two red backs in a snowdrift.

"They did not run away," he said to Pierre. "They only ran. There they are."

He went down to look at them. Their heads and their backs were above the snow. The yoke was crooked. Their noses were together and their eyes were large and wondering.

The three boys dug the snow away from the calves. They dug out the sled. Almanzo straightened the yoke. Then he stood in front of them and said, "Giddap!" while Pierre and Louis pushed them from behind.

The calves climbed onto the road. Almanzo headed them toward the barn. They were glad to go. All the way back to

the barn, they did exactly as Almanzo told them to.

That night Father asked Almanzo if he had had some trouble that afternoon.

"No," Almanzo said. "I just found out I have to break Star and Bright to drive when I ride."

So he did that, in the barnyard.

CHAPTER 4

The Strange Dog

The New York horse-buyers were in the neighborhood. Father gave the four-year-old colts a special grooming. He hoped to sell the colts to the horse-buyers.

Almanzo helped to brush their shining brown sides. He braided their manes and tails. He oiled their hooves till they shone black as Mother's polished stove.

He was careful never to move suddenly and startle them. He talked to them in a gentle, low voice. The colts nuzzled him and arched their necks. Their soft eyes shone. Nothing in the world, Almanzo thought, was as beautiful as a horse.

One evening a horse-buyer came riding into the barnyard. He was new; Father had never seen him before. He was dressed in city clothes, and the ends of his mustache were waxed and twisted. He kept twisting one end of his mustache into a sharper point.

Father led out the colts. They were perfectly matched Morgans, the same size and shape. They had matching white stars on their foreheads.

"Four years old in May," Father said. "Broken to drive double or single. They're high-spirited, full of ginger, and gentle as kittens."

Almanzo listened to every word. Someday he would be trading horses himself.

The buyer inspected the colts closely.

 30

He watched them walk and trot and gallop. At last he offered Father $175 apiece.

Father said he couldn't take less than $225. Almanzo knew that meant Father wanted $200 for each colt. After a long time of arguing over the price, the horse-buyer agreed to pay $200 each. He took a fat wallet out of his pocket and gave Father the money.

The colts were sold, at Father's price.

The buyer would not stay to supper. He rode away, and Father took the money to Mother in the kitchen.

"Must we keep all that money in the house overnight?" Mother exclaimed.

"It's too late to take it to the bank," Father said. "We're safe enough. Nobody but us knows the money's here."

"I declare I shan't sleep a wink!" Mother replied.

Supper that night wasn't as cheerful as usual. There was a dark, heavy feeling about the money in the house. Mother hid it in the pantry. Then she moved it to the linen closet.

Later, mixing up a batch of bread, she worried out loud. "It don't seem as though anybody'd think to look between sheets in a closet, but I declare I— *What's that?*"

They all jumped. They held their breaths and listened.

"Somebody's prowling around this house!" Mother whispered.

But all they could see out the windows was blackness.

Father said he hadn't heard anything at all. But Mother made Royal go look. After a minute, Royal said,

"It's nothing but a stray dog."

 32

"Drive it away!" Mother said.

Royal chased the dog away. Almanzo would have liked to have a dog, but a dog might chase the hens or kill sheep. Mother always said there were enough animals on the place without a dirty dog.

She finished making the bread. Suddenly they all heard a sound on the back porch.

Mother's eyes were big. Was it a robber after the money?

But Royal said, "It's only that dog."

He opened the door. At first they saw nothing. Then they saw a big, skinny dog cringing in the shadows. His ribs showed under his fur.

"Oh, Mother, the poor dog!" Alice cried. "Please, can't I give him just a little bit to eat?"

"Goodness, child, yes!" Mother said.

33

"You can drive him away in the morning, Royal."

Alice set out a pan of food for the dog. He wouldn't come near it while the door was open, but when Almanzo shut the door they heard him chewing. Mother tried the door twice to make sure it was locked. Then they all went to bed.

The next morning Mother had quite a story to tell. During the night, a noise woke her. She sat bolt upright in bed. Father was sound asleep.

The moon was shining and everything was still. Then Mother's blood ran cold. She heard a low, savage growl.

She looked out the window. The strange dog was out in the yard, growling and showing his teeth.

He acted as though somebody was in the trees near the house.

Mother watched. It was too dark under the trees for her to see if anyone was there. But the dog growled savagely at the darkness.

For two hours Mother stood there, watching the dog growl. He walked up and down by the picket fence, showing his teeth.

35

After a long time, he lay down. But he kept his ears pricked, listening. Mother went softly back to bed.

At dawn the dog was gone. They could not find him anywhere. But his tracks were in the yard.

And on the other side of the fence, among the trees, Father found more tracks.

They were the tracks of two men's boots.

Father hitched up the wagon at once and drove to town. He put the money in the bank.

When he came back, he said to Mother, "You were right. We came near to being robbed last night."

In town he had learned that a farmer nearby had sold some horses the week before, and kept the money in the house.

 36

That night robbers broke in and stole the money. The sheriff was looking for them.

"I shouldn't wonder if that horse-buyer had a hand in it," Father said. "Who else knew we had money in the house? But it couldn't be proved. He was at the hotel in Malone last night."

Mother said she would always believe that Providence had sent the strange dog to watch over them. Almanzo thought maybe he stayed because Alice had fed him.

"Maybe he was sent to try us," Mother said. "Maybe the Lord was merciful to us because we were merciful to him."

They never saw the strange dog again.

CHAPTER 5

The Last Fleece

Now the meadows and pastures were velvety with thick grass. The weather was warm.

It was time to shear sheep.

Pierre and Louis came to help, with their fathers, Lazy John and French Joe. First the sheep had to be caught and washed in the river. Their wool was lathered up with soap, and Almanzo and the others scrubbed until the wool was snowy white.

The next morning, Father built a platform in the South Barn. He and Lazy John each caught a sheep and set it up on the platform. They began cutting off the wool with long shears.

The thick mat of wool peeled back all in one piece. The sheep was left in bare pink skin. It would be cool for the summer, and by winter its warm woolly coat would have grown back.

The mat of wool was called a fleece. As Father and Lazy John finished shearing each sheep, Royal rolled up the fleeces and tied them with twine.

Almanzo carried each one up to the loft and laid it on the floor. He ran upstairs and down again as fast as he could, but another fleece was always ready for him. They were so heavy that he could carry only one at a time.

On one of his trips to the loft, Almanzo noticed the barn cat flash past carrying a mouse. He knew she was taking it to her kittens. He wanted to see them, so he ran after her.

Far up under the eaves of the barn, he found the little nest in the hay. Four kittens were mewing inside. The tabby cat curled herself around them, purring proudly. Almanzo marveled at the tiny pink mouths, and the tiny paws with perfect little claws.

When he came back to the sheepfold, six fleeces were waiting.

Father spoke to him sternly. "See to it you keep up with us after this."

"Yes, Father," Almanzo gasped, hurrying.

But he heard Lazy John chuckle. "He can't do it. We'll be through before he is."

Then Father laughed and said, "That's so, John. He can't keep up with us."

 40

Almanzo made up his mind that he'd show them. If he hurried fast enough, he could keep up.

Before noon he had caught up with Royal, and had to wait while a fleece was tied.

"You see," he crowed, "I can keep up with you!"

"Oh no, you can't!" said John. "We'll beat you. We'll be through before you are. Wait and see."

Then they all laughed at Almanzo.

They were laughing when they heard the dinner horn. Father and John finished the sheep they were shearing, and went to the house. Royal tied the last fleece and left it.

Almanzo still had to carry it upstairs. Now he understood why they were laughing. No matter how fast he worked, there

41

would always be a fleece to carry upstairs
after the last sheep was sheared.

Almanzo thought hard. "I won't let
them beat me," he said to himself.

He found a short rope and tied it
around the neck of a sheep that wasn't
sheared. He led the sheep to the stairs.
Step by step he tugged and boosted her
upward.

 42

She bleated all the way, but at last he got her into the loft. He tied her near the fleeces and gave her some hay to keep her quiet. Then he went to dinner.

All that afternoon Lazy John and Royal kept telling him to hurry or they'd beat him. Almanzo answered, "No you won't. I can keep up with you."

Then they laughed at him.

He snatched up every fleece as soon as Royal tied it and hurried upstairs. He raced down again. They all laughed to see him hurrying, and they kept saying, "Oh no, you won't beat us! We'll be through first!"

Just before chore-time, Father and Lazy John raced to shear the last two sheep. Almanzo ran upstairs with Father's fleece, and was back before the last one was ready.

Royal tied it, and then he said: "We're

all through! Almanzo, we beat you! We beat you!"

Royal and John burst into a great roar of laughter. Even Father laughed.

But Almanzo shook his head. "No you haven't beat me," he said. "I've got a fleece upstairs that you haven't sheared yet."

They stopped laughing, surprised. At that very minute the sheep in the loft cried out, "Baa-aa-aa!"

Almanzo shouted, "There's the fleece! I've got it upstairs and you haven't sheared it! I beat you!"

John and Royal stared at him with open mouths. They looked so funny that Almanzo couldn't stop laughing. Father roared with laughter.

"The joke's on you, John!" Father shouted. "He laughs best who laughs last!"

 44

Starlight

Spring passed quickly into summer. Corn grew waist-high in the fields. Potato plants sent out their frothy white blossoms, and yellow blossoms appeared in the pumpkin patch.

Almanzo had a little pig all his own. She was so small that he fed her, at first, with a rag dipped in milk. But soon she learned to drink. He kept her in a pen in the shade, because young pigs grow best in the shade. He fed her all she could eat. She was growing fast.

Almanzo was growing fast, too—but not

fast enough. He drank all the milk he could hold. At mealtimes he filled his plate so full that he could not eat it all. Father looked stern because he left food on his plate.

"What's the matter, son?" Father asked. "Your eyes bigger than your stomach?"

Then Almanzo tried to swallow a little more.

He did not tell anyone he was trying to grow up faster so he could help break the colts.

Every day Father took the two-year-old colts out. He trained them to start and stop. He taught them to wear bridles and harness, and not to be afraid of anything. Pretty soon he would hitch each one up with a gentle old horse, and teach it to pull a light cart.

Almanzo wasn't allowed to help. He wasn't even allowed to set foot in the barnyard while Father was working with the colts.

Almanzo knew he wouldn't frighten the horses. He would never teach them to jump or run away. But Father wouldn't trust a nine-year-old.

That year one of the mares, Beauty, had the prettiest colt Almanzo had ever seen. He had a perfect white star on his forehead. Almanzo named him Starlight.

Starlight spent his days running in the pasture with Beauty. One day, when Father was in town, Almanzo went into the pasture.

Beauty lifted her head and watched him coming. The little colt ran behind her. Almanzo stood perfectly still.

After a while Starlight peeked at him, under Beauty's neck. Almanzo didn't move. Little by little the colt stretched its neck toward Almanzo. He stared at Almanzo with wide, wondering eyes.

Beauty nuzzled his back and swished her tail. Then she took a step and bit on a clump of grass. Starlight stood trembling, looking at Almanzo.

The colt took one step, then another. He was so near that Almanzo could have touched him.

But he didn't. He didn't move.

Starlight took a step nearer. Almanzo didn't even breathe.

Suddenly the colt turned and ran back to its mother. Slowly, Almanzo let out his breath.

He heard Eliza Jane calling him.

"Ma-a-a-nzo!"

She had seen him. That night she told Father about it.

Almanzo said he hadn't done a thing, honest he hadn't. But Father's eyes were stern.

"Let me catch you fooling with that colt again and I'll tan your jacket," Father said. "That's too good a colt to be spoiled. I won't have you teaching it tricks that I'll have to train out of it."

All the rest of the summer Almanzo thought about Starlight. He remembered the bright look in the little colt's eyes.

49

Everywhere he went, he remembered those eyes.

He was thinking about Starlight one morning when Father announced it was time to go berry-picking. Everyone cheered. Picking berries was a treat.

They drove far into the mountains, where the wild huckleberries and blue-berries grew. The woods were full of laughter and song. Other families had come to pick berries also.

There was a sweet smell in the air. The sun shone down on the blue-black berries. Birds fluttered and fought in the berry patches. Once two blue jays attacked Alice's sunbonnet. Almanzo had to beat them off.

And once, when he had wandered a little way off from the others, Almanzo met a black bear.

 50

The bear was standing on its hind legs near a cedar tree. It stuffed berries into its mouth with both furry paws.

Almanzo stood stock-still. So did the bear.

Almanzo stared. The bear stared back at him. Its paws froze halfway to its mouth.

Its eyes were like two black beads. Almanzo kept looking into those black eyes.

He held his breath.

All at once the bear dropped to all fours. It went waddling away into the woods.

Almanzo could breathe again. All in all, he'd rather look into Starlight's eyes.

CHAPTER 7

Mr. Thompson's Pocketbook

The summer slipped away quickly, and then the fall. Almanzo was almost ten now. But he still wasn't old enough to help with the colts.

He was old enough, though, to help Father bale the hay that winter. He stayed home from school and worked with Father in the barnyard all day long.

That night he sat at the supper table, thinking about the money the baled hay would earn. He was thinking so hard that he thought out loud, without meaning to.

"Thirty bales to a load," he said, "at two dollars a bale. That's sixty dollars a lo—"

Mother and Father stared at him.

"Mercy on us, listen to the boy!" Mother said.

"Well, well, son!" said Father. "I see you've been studying to some purpose." He drank the rest of his tea, set down the saucer, and looked at Almanzo. "Learning is best put into practice. What say you ride to town with me tomorrow, and sell that load of hay?"

"Oh, yes! Please, Father!" Almanzo almost shouted.

Once again he did not have to go to school. He rode in the wagon on top of the bales, enjoying the blue sky and the good smell of the hay.

Just beyond the bridge over Trout River, Almanzo saw a small black thing lying beside the road. When the wagon passed, he leaned over the edge of the hay to look. It was a pocketbook.

He yelled to Father. Father stopped the horses to let him climb down and pick it up. It was a fat, black wallet.

Father handed Almanzo the reins while he looked inside the pocketbook. A thrill went through Almanzo. He was driving, all by himself!

"There's fifteen hundred dollars here," Father said wonderingly. "Now who does it belong to? He's a man who's afraid of banks, or he wouldn't carry so much money around. You can see by the creases in the bills, he's carried them some time. Now who's suspicious, and stingy, and sold something valuable lately?"

 54

Almanzo didn't know. But Father didn't expect him to answer. The horses went around a curve in the road as well as if Father had been driving them.

"Thompson!" Father said. "He sold some land last fall. He's afraid of banks, and he's so stingy he'd skin a flea for its hide. Thompson's the man!"

He put the pocketbook in his pocket and took the reins from Almanzo. "We'll see if we can find him in town," he said.

Father drove first to the Livery Stable. Sure enough, Father let Almanzo sell the hay. He stood back and did not say anything, while Almanzo showed the liveryman that the hay was good and clean.

"How much do you want for it?" the liveryman asked.

"Two dollars and a quarter a bale," Almanzo said.

But the liveryman said he wouldn't pay a penny over two dollars.

"All right, I'll take two dollars," Almanzo said quickly.

The liveryman looked at Father. He asked Almanzo why he had priced the hay at two dollars and a quarter in the first place.

"Well," Almanzo said, "if I'd asked two, you wouldn't have paid but one seventy-five."

The liveryman laughed. "That's a smart boy of yours," he told Father.

He counted out the sixty dollars and gave it to Almanzo. Almanzo had sold that load of hay all by himself.

Father went to do some shopping at the general store. He gave Almanzo the pocketbook and told him to look for Mr. Thompson. Almanzo walked down the

 56

street, thinking about how glad Mr. Thompson would be to see it again.

At last he saw Mr. Thompson's team in front of Mr. Paddock's wagon shop. He opened the door of the long, low building and went in.

Mr. Paddock and Mr. Thompson were standing by the stove, talking. Almanzo waited patiently for them to finish.

Mr. Thompson was arguing about the price of a new wagon. Mr. Paddock figured the cost with his big pencil. Mr. Thompson frowned and complained, and finally he said he'd come back if he couldn't find a better deal anywhere else. He turned to the door.

"Did you lose a pocketbook?" Almanzo asked him.

Mr. Thompson jumped. He clapped a hand to his pocket.

"Yes, I have!" he shouted. "Fifteen hundred dollars in it, too. What about it? What do you know about it?"

"Is this it?" Almanzo asked.

Mr. Thompson snatched the pocketbook. "Yes, yes, yes, that's it!" he said. He opened the pocketbook and counted the money.

He counted all the bills twice. He looked exactly like a man skinning a flea for its hide.

At last he sighed with relief. "Well," he said, "this durn boy didn't steal any of it."

Almanzo's face was hot as fire. He wanted to hit Mr. Thompson.

Mr. Thompson put his skinny hand into his pocket and pulled out a nickel.

"Here," he said, putting it in Almanzo's hand.

Almanzo was so angry he couldn't see.

 58

He hated Mr. Thompson. That mean old man had as good as called him a thief. Almanzo didn't want his old nickel. Suddenly he knew what to say.

"Here," he said, handing the nickel back. "Keep your nickel. I can't change it."

Mr. Thompson's mean face turned red. Mr. Paddock was furious. He shook his fist under Mr. Thompson's nose.

"Don't you call this boy a thief, Thompson!" Mr. Paddock roared. "When he brings you back your fifteen hundred dollars! Call him a thief and hand him a nickel, will you?"

Mr. Thompson stepped backward, but Mr. Paddock followed him.

"You measly skinflint," Mr. Paddock said. "A good, honest, decent little chap and you— No! You hand him a hundred of that money, and do it quick! No, two hundred! Two hundred dollars, I say!"

Mr. Thompson tried to say something, and so did Almanzo. But Mr. Paddock's fists clenched. The muscles of his arms bulged. He towered over Mr. Thompson.

Mr. Thompson nervously counted out some bills. He held them out to Almanzo.

"Now get out!" Mr. Paddock said. Mr. Thompson shoved the bills into Almanzo's hand and hurried outside.

Almanzo hardly knew what to say. He felt strange about taking all that money. But Mr. Paddock went with him to find Father, and told him all about it. After a while, Father said that Almanzo could keep the money.

Almanzo stared at the bills. Two hundred dollars. That was as much as the horse-buyer paid for one of Father's colts.

He told Father he wanted to put

the money in the bank.

"That's the place to put money," Father agreed. "Well, well, well, two hundred dollars! I was twice your age before I had so much."

"So was I," said Mr. Paddock. "Older than that!"

They went to the bank, and Almanzo opened an account. He got a little book with $200 written in it, to tell him how much was in his account. The money would be there waiting for him, whenever he wanted to use it.

Almanzo knew just what he wanted to do. He would buy a little colt of his own. He could break it himself; he could teach it everything. He would not have to wait until he was grown-up.

But this was not the end of that exciting day.

 62

CHAPTER 8

Almanzo Chooses

Mr. Paddock was waiting outside the bank. He told Father he had something in mind.

"I've been meaning to speak to you about it for some time," he said. "About this boy of yours. You ever think of making a wheelwright out of him?"

Almanzo was surprised. Father shook his head slowly.

"Well, no," he said, "I can't say as I ever did."

Mr. Paddock asked Father to think about it. He said wagon-making was a

63

growing business. He was getting more customers all the time.

"I've got no sons of my own," Mr. Paddock explained. "And you've got two. You'll have to think about starting Almanzo out in life, before long. Apprentice him to me, and I'll treat the boy right. It's worth thinking about."

"Yes," Father said slowly. "It's worth thinking about."

All the way home Father was very quiet. Almanzo did not say anything, either. So much had happened. His thoughts were all mixed up.

He thought about the busy, cheerful, warm wagon-shop. He had often envied Mr. Paddock's workmen. He loved their tools, and the way they shaved long strips of wood off a board. He would like to saw and whittle and paint, as they did.

 64

And if he was Mr. Paddock's apprentice, he wouldn't have to go to school.

Then he felt the small bankbook in his pocket. He thought about a colt. He wanted a colt with slender legs and large, wondering eyes, like Starlight's. He wanted to teach the little colt everything, as he had taught Star and Bright.

It was supper-time when they got home. They told Mother all about Mr. Thompson and the money. Mother said you could have knocked her over with a feather.

Then Father told her the rest. He told about Mr. Paddock wanting to take Almanzo on as an apprentice.

Mother's brown eyes snapped. Her cheeks turned as red as her red wool dress.

"I never heard of such a thing!" she said. "Well, the sooner Mr. Paddock gets

65

that out of his head, the better!"

Father tried to calm her down. "He looks on it as a good opening for the boy," he explained.

But Mother was mad as an angry hen. "Well!" she snapped. "A pretty pass the world's coming to, if any man thinks it's a step up in the world to leave a good farm and go to town!"

"I feel the same way you do," said Father. "But the boy'll have to decide. We can keep him here on the farm by law till he's twenty-one, but it won't do any good if he's wanting to go." He shook his head. If Almanzo wanted to go to town, Father said, it would be better to apprentice him to Paddock.

Almanzo went on eating. The good taste of roast pork and applesauce filled every corner of his mouth. But all the time he was listening hard.

Father looked at him. "Son," he said soberly, "you heard what Paddock said. What do you say about it?"

Almanzo didn't know what to say. He hadn't supposed he could say anything. He would have to do whatever Father said.

"Well, son, you think about it," said Father. "I want you should make up your own mind. With Paddock, you'd have an easy life, in some ways. You wouldn't be out in all kinds of weather. Cold winter nights, you could lie snug in bed and not worry about young stock freezing. Likely you'd always have plenty to eat and wear and money in the bank."

"James!" Mother said.

"That's the truth, and we must be fair about it," Father answered. "But there's

67

the other side, too, Almanzo."

His voice was low and calm, but Almanzo could tell that every word Father said was important.

"You'd have to depend on other folks in town," Father told him. "Everything you got, you'd get from other folks."

Almanzo thought about Mr. Paddock trying to sell that wagon to Mr. Thompson. Mr. Paddock had to please a mean old man like Mr. Thompson, or lose the sale.

Father went on. "A farmer depends on himself, and the land and the weather. If you're a farmer, you raise what you eat, you raise what you wear, and you keep warm with wood out of your own timber. You work hard, but you work as you please, and no man can tell you to go or come. You'll be free and independent, son, on a farm."

Almanzo squirmed. Father was looking

at him too hard, and so was Mother.
Almanzo did not want to live inside walls
and please people he didn't like, and
never have horses and cows and fields.

He wanted to be just like Father.

"You take your time, son," Father said.
"Think it over. You make up your mind
what you want."

Almanzo found his voice. "Father!"

"Yes, son?"

"Can I really tell you what I want?"

"Yes, son," Father said warmly.

Almanzo took a deep breath.

"I want a colt," he said. "Could I buy a colt all my own with some of that two hundred dollars, and would you let me break him?"

Father began to smile. He looked at Mother, and she was smiling too.

"Son," Father said, "you leave that money in the bank."

Almanzo felt everything sinking down inside him. And then, suddenly, the whole world was a great, shining glow of light. For Father went on:

"If it's a colt you want, I'll give you Starlight."

"Father!" Almanzo gasped. "For my very own?"

 70

"Yes, son," Father said. "You can break him, and drive him, and when he's a four-year-old you can sell him or keep him, as you like. First thing tomorrow morning, you can begin."

Almanzo's heart soared. Starlight!

He was not yet ten years old, and the most beautiful colt in the world was his very own. He wouldn't trade Starlight for all the wagon-shops in the world.

The LAURA *Years*

By Laura Ingalls Wilder

Illustrated by Garth Williams

———

LITTLE HOUSE IN THE BIG WOODS

LITTLE HOUSE ON THE PRAIRIE

FARMER BOY

ON THE BANKS OF PLUM CREEK

BY THE SHORES OF SILVER LAKE

THE LONG WINTER

LITTLE TOWN ON THE PRAIRIE

THESE HAPPY GOLDEN YEARS

THE FIRST FOUR YEARS

The ROSE *Years*
By Roger Lea MacBride

———

The CAROLINE *Years*
By Maria D. Wilkes

———

Other LITTLE HOUSE *titles you may enjoy*: